Cora's Tree

A Storm Ketchum Tale

by

Garrett Dennis

This story is a work of fiction. The Kinnakeet Boatyard, the Sea Dog Scuba Center, and HatterasMann Realty are fictitious. Other businesses and organizations, locales, scientific and religious references, and historical figures and events are real, but may be used fictitiously.

CORA'S TREE
Storm Ketchum Tale #3
ISBN: 978-1543277678 (1543277675)

~ *Author's Note* ~

Greetings, and welcome to my world! I'm the author of the **Storm Ketchum Adventures**, a series of full-length Outer Banks mystery and adventure novels that begins with the novel ***PORT STARBIRD***.

The story you're about to read is a Storm Ketchum Tale. The **Storm Ketchum Tales** are short stories that accompany the Storm Ketchum Adventures. They can be read along with, or independently of, the full-length Adventures (though you might not get some of the 'inside jokes' if you don't read the Adventures first).

Chronologically, this story (which is Tale #3) takes place between ***The Sad Blue Boat*** (Tale #2) and ***PORT STARBIRD*** (Adventure #1).

Please visit **www.GarrettDennis.com** if you want to learn more about the Adventures, the Tales, and Ketch's world. That site also contains information on how to connect with me on social media and by e-mail, and on how to sign up for my VIP reader list.

And now – sit back and enjoy!

The Outer Banks

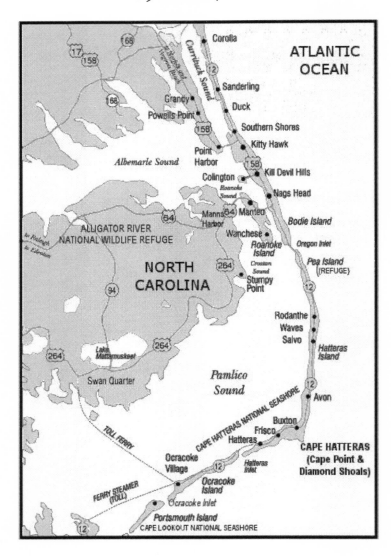

~ Cora's Tree ~

*I*t was Halloween again – and for the first time in a long while, Ketch actually had somewhere to go tonight. Somewhere, that is, where he'd been invited and people were expecting him. Who knows, some of them may even be looking forward to his arrival, he thought, though that might be stretching things a bit. He'd made numerous acquaintances since he'd moved here, but there were only a handful (if that) whom he could legitimately count as friends.

He'd done his civic duty earlier regarding the neighborhood trick-or-treaters – all eight of them, as it had turned out – and he'd been generous with the handouts, but the candy bowl was still half-full. It was only a little after seven now, but no one had come to the door in the past half-hour. He guessed he could bring the leftover candy to the party. He certainly wouldn't leave it out on the front porch, as he might have back North. That would be asking for trouble in this climate, specifically of the cockroach variety.

There were safer alternatives to begging treats door-to-door these days, like trunk-or-treating and indoor events at schools and churches. Plus it was no longer tourist season, and since many of the neighboring homes hereabouts were vacation rentals, children were simply scarcer at this time of year. Though hundreds of thousands of vacationers typically visited the Outer Banks annually, that mostly happened during the summer. The permanent, year-round population of Hatteras Island numbered maybe four thousand, tops, in all seven island villages combined. So tonight's paltry turnout wasn't surprising.

He wanted to be at the party by eight or so, and it would take at least twenty minutes to drive down to the Captain's condo in Hatteras village, so he supposed he'd better get going. Jack had gone outside just a short time ago and was set for the evening, and Ketch was already wearing most of the pirate costume he'd rented for the occasion.

He quickly double-checked his appearance in the dresser mirror. His salt-and-pepper beard was closely cropped the way he liked it, and he saw nothing that could be potentially embarrassing except for maybe his hair. He started to lift his comb to rectify that, but then made like the Fonz and put it back in his pocket. He'd decided to wear the bandana that matched his sash (the tricorn hat that had also come with the costume being a bit over the top, in his opinion), so why bother? Jack, who was lying on a nearby throw rug, raised his head and gave him a funny look.

"Don't worry, boy," he said to the dog. "I'm okay. I'm just happy, that's all. *Happy Days*, remember? You've seen that old show." He smiled and gave his most faithful friend a quick rub on the head. He'd found a marathon on one of those rerun channels last week during a storm, and he'd left the TV on for most of that rainy day while he'd puttered indoors.

He really *was* happy, he realized. In the past, he'd felt this way so infrequently for so many years that it had been almost shocking when it had sometimes happened. But after being here in Avon for two and a half years now, he was starting to take the feeling for granted. No, two and a half years in this house plus three months of house-hunting before that, so two years and nine months. Finally moving here for good had been one of the best decisions he'd ever made.

With the candy bowl in hand and a light jacket tossed over his shoulder, Ketch turned off all the lights save one for Jack, and bade the dog farewell. He didn't really need the jacket right now, but he supposed it was possible he might want it later. He hadn't been living here long enough yet for his blood to thin like that of the natives, and he was plenty warm in his long-sleeved swashbuckler shirt, knee breeches, and Caribbean pirate boots.

Working the pedals with those oversized boots on his feet was a tad problematic at first, but he managed to navigate his pickup down North End Road and then Harbor Road. By the time he reached Highway 12 at the end of that road, he'd gotten the hang of it.

There was hardly any traffic, so he allowed himself the luxury of a leisurely drive to Buxton, the next village down the island's one and only two-lane highway. Driving well under the speed limit with his window rolled down, he breathed deeply of the salty air from the Atlantic just beyond the dunes to his left while enjoying the nighttime views of Pamlico Sound to his right. This was a narrow part of the island, and the water was only a short walk from the road in both directions.

After passing the iconic Cape Hatteras Lighthouse, he drove through Buxton, which had been called Cape in the old days, and continued on toward Frisco, which had originally been known as Trent. The names had changed with the coming of postal service in the late nineteenth century. His town, Avon, had once been called Kinnakeet – but Hatteras village, his ultimate destination tonight at the southern end of the island, had kept its name.

Along the way, he thought of Svetlana and Sergey, the children he'd aided a year and a half ago after Jack had ferreted out their makeshift refuge in Buxton Woods. They'd been part of a Russian family that had traveled to Cuba on business. Their mother had attempted to desert her abusive husband and escape with them to America in an old boat she'd bought on the sly, but her plan had fallen apart at the seams. She'd ended up in custody back in Cuba, and the boat with the children on it had been carried by the current and blown ashore on the beach near the lighthouse. The desperate and frightened children had been lucky to survive the journey, and luckier still that Ketch had been the one who'd found them.

They hadn't been able to speak a word of

English at the time, but Ketch knew they'd been learning, as he'd been getting a postcard from them once a month for the past year. The mother's well-off friends in Miami's Russian community, whom Ketch had contacted in lieu of the authorities, had taken them in and managed to hang onto them during the minor political storm that had followed. He'd spoken with the hosts by phone several times and followed the progress of the case on the news. Their resourceful mother's second escape attempt had succeeded, and improbably as it had seemed to him throughout, they'd all been granted asylum in the end despite the protests of the father, the Cuban government, and even the Russian government, which had also gotten in on the act.

He'd recently learned that the three of them, along with their Miami hosts, would be vacationing in Washington, D.C., during spring break – and that they were planning on a brief stayover in Avon on the way, at the kids' insistence. He'd assured them that he'd provide accommodations for them, but he didn't think he could handle that many houseguests at *Port Starbird*, at least not in the style to which they may have become accustomed in Miami. And there were no hotels in Avon other than the Avon Motel, which was modest at best.

So he was planning on renting one of the newer beach houses for them all. Five bedrooms would be adequate, so it wouldn't need to be one of those ten- or twelve-bedroom monstrosities, and it shouldn't be prohibitively expensive at that time of year. But even if it was, it would be worth it to see those two little troopers again.

He should probably make those arrangements sooner than later, he decided, and give some thought as well to choosing a couple of historic sites to show them during their visit. The lighthouse was an obvious choice, as was the Chicamacomico Life Saving Station and museum up in Rodanthe, where the old-time surfmen had bravely rescued shipwreck victims from the Graveyard of the Atlantic at great personal risk – though that might be too time-consuming, especially since he'd of course have to take them to the Graveyard of the Atlantic Museum in Hatteras, where their sad blue boat was on display outside.

Speaking of tourist attractions, he was now approaching the housing development at Brigands' Bay in Frisco. That put him in mind of the Cora Tree, which was a sizeable old live oak at the center of that community that had been split by lightning a long time ago. The tree was in the middle of a street there, and he'd heard the road divided and went around the tree – and as was often the case hereabouts, there were local legends that also swirled around that tree.

Oddly enough, despite the many times he'd vacationed on this island before he'd retired, and even though he was now living here full-time, he'd never gotten around to visiting the tree. But he had looked up its location one time online, and he thought he could remember how to find it.

So why not just make a quick stop right now? He knew there was nothing else to see or do there beyond the tree itself – and he also knew that it probably didn't much matter what time he showed up at the party. Knowing the Captain, there would be plenty of other guests. Truth be told, he doubted he'd be missed right away, if ever. And though it was dark out now, the moon was almost full and there might be streetlights, and he had a flashlight in the glove box in case he needed one.

He slowed and kept his eyes peeled for Buccaneer Drive, which he'd have to make a right turn onto off Highway 12. And after that came, what was it? Ah yes, Snug Harbor Drive was the road the tree was on. Okay, there was Buccaneer...

Ketch had no trouble finding the correct street – but when he did, he saw that there was more than one big tree occupying the median between the two lanes. He drove down one side of the street and back up the other. It must be this one right here, he thought. It was the only one that looked like it could have been struck by lightning. He parked the truck, retrieved his flashlight from the glove box, and stepped out.

Legend had it that an accused witch named Cora had caused her name to be burned into the tree back in the early seventeen hundreds. And Ketch remembered reading that after all this time, it could be difficult to spot what remained of the name. Ambient light or no, he was glad he'd brought the flashlight.

It didn't seem to help much, though. He panned the light around the tree's trunk a couple of times without success. Was the name smaller than what he was expecting to see? Did he have the right tree? He moved closer to the trunk and squinted mightily as he slowly panned again.

"Would you be looking for the famous Cora's name, sir?" a voice behind him demurely inquired.

Startled, Ketch quickly turned, almost dropping the flashlight in the process. A woman had apparently crept up behind him without him noticing.

"Why yes, er, miss, yes I am," he said. Her face, at least, which was about all he could see of her, looked to be on the younger side. She was wearing a plain gray ankle-length dress with long sleeves. The dress was fronted by a white apron, and a plain white bonnet covered her head.

"Would you be wanting me to show you it, sir?" she asked. Ketch mutely nodded and she moved closer to the tree, forcing him to step aside. "Stand a wee bit farther back, sir, and aim your torch here," she said, touching a spot on the trunk.

He did as she instructed, she traced the outline with her finger – and there it was, plain as day now that he knew where to look and what to look for. It wasn't smaller than he'd expected, but rather larger. And though it had apparently faded significantly or some of the bark had grown back, it was definitely there.

"Thank you," he said.

"You are most welcome, sir," the woman responded with a slight curtsy. "Do you know the story of this oak, sir?"

He thought he did, but he also thought it might be interesting to hear a local tell it. "Some of it, yes, but I'd like to know more," he said. The woman seemed pleased.

"'Twas in the year of our Lord 1705," she began. "Cora came carrying a wee babe with her. She stayed at a hut not far from this very spot. Folks here left her be, but there came misfortunes. She touched a cow and it went dry, a boy who laughed at her babe fell sick, and no fisher save herself could catch enough fish."

Ketch was listening, but he was somewhat distracted by the woman's manner of speech. He hadn't heard anything quite like it on the islands, except for perhaps the old Hoi Toider brogue that was still spoken by some on Ocracoke, the next island down the Banks. But it wasn't exactly like that, either.

"Well," she went on, "along about that time came Captain Eli Blood of the town of Salem in the colony of Massachusetts. His brig, that were named the *Susan G.*, foundered on the shoals, and he and his crew stayed here to await word from the brig's owner. While he waited, a dead man washed up on the beach with the Mark of The Beast burned into his forehead, and there were

9

womanish footprints nearby. And then when the Captain learned of Cora and her misdeeds, he decided to test her to see if she were a witch."

Now *there* was certainly a stroke of bad luck for old Cora, Ketch thought. The digits '666' on the dead body's forehead (he hadn't heard that bit before), plus the arrival of a man who'd probably been present at the Salem witch trials of 1692, was a recipe for disaster if there ever was one.

"First he had her bound with ropes and thrown in the sound, and then he tried to cut her hair. She floated in the water, and he said he were unable to cut because the hair were tough as wire rope, and that were two signs of witchery. Then he pricked his own finger and stirred his blood in a bowl of water, so as to read it. The blood in the water, too, said she were a witch."

"That's ridiculous," Ketch said.

"I heartily agree, sir! And then the Captain remanded her to this very tree to be tied with her babe in her arms, and kindling were bundled to burn them. But another captain by the name of Tom Smith said he could not abide such an execution and the mainland court should rule instead."

"So there was at least one sensible person, then," Ketch remarked.

"Indeed, sir. And then while Captain Smith and Captain Blood discussed, they say the babe became a cat with green eyes and red mouth, and ran off into the woods. And the sun were covered by a

10

great dark cloud and lightning struck the tree and there were smoke. When the smoke cleared, Cora were gone, leaving behind the rope and kindling and her name burned into this tree. And so the story ends," the woman concluded.

"Do you believe that ending?" Ketch asked her. She only smiled in response. "Poor Cora," he said. "It's a shame women used to be treated so unfairly. It's always amazed me that people would turn on their midwives and healers and such the way they did, when they had such need of their services back then. But I guess that's what happens when you combine ignorance and superstition and religious zealotry... I wonder what really happened to Cora, if there was such a person."

"Oh, there were, sir, of that I am certain. And she were a cunning woman, as you said, but she were not witchy. And though she did not burn that day, she surely did in a time to come."

"You're probably right." Ketch thought for a moment. "But you know, I've heard another story, one that says this name was carved into the tree by the fiance of a girl named Cora who lived here fifty or so years ago. But that story isn't quite as interesting, is it?" he smiled.

"No, sir, it is not. Nor is it the truest tale."

"Are you going to a Halloween party?" Ketch asked her. "I'm on my way to one down in Hatteras," he added by way of explaining his own outlandish attire – which she so far hadn't remarked on.

And she didn't now. "I am sorry, sir, but I know not of what you speak." She looked past him over his shoulder then and said, "Oh! I must take my leave now. Good eve to you, kind sir."

Ketch swiveled for a moment to see what had caught her attention. When he turned back around, she was gone.

He looked about in consternation. She was nowhere in sight. Where could she have gotten to so quickly, and so soundlessly? He recalled that he hadn't heard her approaching earlier, either. Had she ever really been here at all? Had he imagined the encounter, or hallucinated it? Was there something wrong with him – or with her?

The hairs on the back of his neck suddenly standing on end, he beat a hasty retreat to his truck, fired it up, and took off. He wasn't panicked enough to drive recklessly – especially tonight of all nights, when there might still be trick-or-treaters afoot in the dark – but he didn't start to relax until he was back on Highway 12 and had put Brigands' Bay in the rearview mirror.

And now that he had, he felt silly. He wasn't a superstitious man, and yet he'd allowed himself to be spooked by that woman. He thought again about her peculiar speech and mannerisms.

'Good eve', she'd said to him, he recalled. Tonight was Halloween, or All Hallows' Eve, the one night of the year when pre-Christian pagans had believed the souls of the departed could return to their homes seeking hospitality. Hence the tradition of 'guising', now called trick-or-treating, in which people had disguised themselves to represent the souls of the dead and gone begging from house to house, where they'd received offerings of food given in hopes of good fortune from the spirits.

Atypically distracted from the island scenery and starry skies he ordinarily enjoyed so much, he autopiloted the pickup toward Hatteras village. She'd also spoken as if she were taking what had supposedly happened to the eighteenth-century Cora as a personal affront, and she'd seemed quite certain that Cora had in fact existed and been mistreated by that demented ship's captain from Salem, as well as perhaps by the legal system of that era. Could she have been that Cora herself, returning on this night to her former home in search of succor? She'd seemed satisfied at the end of their encounter. Had his sympathetic reaction to her story appeased her spirit?

Although Ketch didn't consider himself superstitious (he again reminded himself), he did believe that there was more to life, the universe, and everything (to paraphrase a favorite author of his) than met the eye. We don't know everything yet, he thought, not by a long shot, and we probably never will. Maybe there *are* such things as ghosts...

But tonight, back there at Cora's Tree? Nonsense, he decided, until proven otherwise. As a former scientist, he was conditioned to search for a logical explanation first and foremost, rather than automatically resorting to the supernatural.

So how could the woman's sudden disappearance be rationalized scientifically? Well, maybe she'd been wearing soft shoes or slippers (he hadn't noticed) and she'd simply hurried off when his back had been turned, and he hadn't been able to see her in the dark. But the moon was almost full tonight, so why hadn't he been able to see her? Maybe his pupils had been dilated by the flashlight he'd been using, so his surroundings had temporarily appeared darker to him. Yes, that was probably all it had been. Still, it would be interesting to hear what his friend the Captain might make of it.

He had a name, this friend, but Ketch just called him 'Captain'. He was a semi-retired charter captain who berthed his boat at the Kinnakeet Boatyard near where Ketch lived, and the salty dog had been the first real friend Ketch had made upon moving to Avon. Ketch had started serving as mate on his occasional fishing charters this past summer, even though he himself had never fished and had no desire to start now. He just liked driving the boat and spending time on the water.

Before he knew it, Ketch was pulling into the parking lot of the Captain's condominium complex on the outskirts of Hatteras. The old mariner was out on his covered deck, which Ketch saw had been gussied up with strings of orange lights for Halloween, along with some tiki torches for the mosquitoes. The tacky skipper's cap the man habitually wore was easy to spot. And though Ketch knew he technically wasn't in costume, the rest of the outfit he was wearing tonight made him look a lot like the Skipper from that old *Gilligan's Island* TV series.

"Ahoy there, swabbie!" he thundered at Ketch over the blaring reggae music and general hubbub. "Where the hell you been?" A couple of dogs started barking somewhere within the neighboring units. "Did you finally get some action or somethin'?"

Ketch left his jacket behind in the truck, but remembered the candy. "Hello, Captain," he replied in a normal tone of voice when he'd gotten close enough to not have to yell. There were a lot of people at this party, more than he'd expected, and even more inside than out. But he could see that most of them were costumed, like him, so he didn't feel any more out of place than he would have anyway. He didn't generally do well with crowds. "No, no action," he said. "But I did meet a woman on the way down here."

"You dawg! Do tell! But first, lemme get you a beer." The Captain put two fingers in his mouth and whistled loudly at a pirate wench standing near a keg. "Ahoy there, Kitty," he called, "three beers!"

"Kitty?" Ketch inquired.

"Yeah, you hadn't met her yet. I asked her out the other night over at the Froggy Dog."

"You just started going out with her, and you're already ordering her around?"

"She's a dang barmaid! So she's used to waitin' on me. *My girlfriend is a waitress, my girlfriend is a waitress*," he began singing. "You remember that one? The Iguanas!"

The wench arrived promptly with three Solo cups and delivered them to the Captain in what Ketch thought was a sarcastic, though benign, manner. Then she sashayed away, looking back over her shoulder to make sure he was watching. She was shapely and attractive, but looked to be at least in her mid-forties - a bit long in the tooth for the Captain, given what Ketch knew of some of his past conquests.

The Captain passed two of the cups to Ketch. "Why three?" Ketch asked, taking them.

"'Cause you got some catchin' up to do! All right now, you set yourself and your candy on down here and tell me 'bout this lady a yours," the Captain said, directing Ketch to the only vacant seat at a nearby picnic table. "'Scuse me, darlin','" he then said to a girl sitting opposite Ketch. Taking her by the elbow, he escorted her to her feet and sat down in her place. She looked to be three sheets to the wind already, and was apparently oblivious to what the Captain had just done. Ketch watched her weave her way unsteadily toward the entrance to the condo.

"Aren't you worried someone might make a complaint about all this noise?" Ketch asked the

Captain.

"Naw! And I'll tell you why. See if you can follow me here. Who's the one does the complainin' 'bout a loud party? Somebody that didn't get invited, right? So I invited everybody in the whole dang place!"

Ketch took that to mean all of the condos in this complex – but who knew, from the looks of things he might have invited some other neighbors as well. And then some others who weren't neighbors, of course, such as himself.

"Good thinking," Ketch said.

"You're lookin' spiffy. Who're you supposed to be, Blackbeard's accountant?" the Captain laughed. "I'm just kiddin', you look good. It's no wonder you got the ladies followin' you around!"

"Right. Speaking of ladies, have you seen Kari yet?" Ketch inquired.

"Nope, nor Len. But they both said they was comin'. Mario too, but he ain't here yet neither."

Ketch was ambivalent about Mario. He seemed like a jovial and friendly sort, but Ketch had heard he was somewhat of an outlaw. Len was an okay guy, though. They were both young and both staying at the boatyard, Len on a rented houseboat and Mario on his old trawler.

"How come you're askin' after Kari?" the Captain asked. "You gettin' sweet on her now? I wouldn't blame you if you was. She's a looker, all right. Say, ain't you workin' for her now?"

"Yes, I'm assisting with the pool work for her

diving classes. And I'm only asking after her because that would make two people I know at this party."

Kari Gellhorn, a PADI instructor who owned and operated the Sea Dog Scuba Center in Avon, was indeed a looker, especially considering that she must be pushing forty. He being a certified divemaster (a level below instructor), Ketch was pack-muling for her classes and helping with the training exercises in exchange for free air fills and other minor perks at the shop rather than for money, because he knew she was having trouble making ends meet. But she had a boyfriend. That would be Mick, a no-good layabout in Ketch's opinion – but that was none of his business.

"Oh yeah? That's all? Then how come your face is changin' colors like one a them little lizards?" the Captain teased. "Never mind. Tell me who you met tonight."

Ketch cleared his throat and took a drink. "Well," he began, "I decided to pay a visit to the Cora Tree in Frisco on my way here. I assume you've heard of it?" The Captain nodded. "There was no particular reason, I'd just never seen it before and I happened to think of it." Ketch then proceeded to recap the incident, leaving nothing out – including his irrational panic at the end of it. The Captain didn't interrupt (much), to Ketch's surprise.

"Whoa!" the Captain exclaimed when Ketch had finished. "Sounds like it mighta been the ghost

18

a Cora her own self!"

"No, I don't think so. I was probably just blinded by the flashlight, and that's why I didn't see her walk away. But I found it disconcerting at the time."

"There you go again, with them big words a yours. You mean you was spooked, right? Well, I don't blame you t'all. I woulda turned tail and run too, if I seen a ghost all dolled up like that and talkin' funny and all."

"I don't think she was a spirit, Captain. This is how folklore legends get started, you know. People see something they don't know how to logically explain, so they make superstitious assumptions, and then the story keeps growing with the telling. Kind of like that cobia you caught back in August, which was almost the size of a great white the last time you told that story," Ketch added with a twinkle in his eye.

"Ha! You got me there. Well, it's still a pretty good yarn, even if it don't have big fish nor bar fights nor loose women. Not as good as my own tall tales, though, a course." The Captain sat up a little straighter and looked past Ketch out into the parking lot. "What'd you say that gal looked like again?"

Ketch began reiterating how the woman was dressed. But he didn't get to finish.

"Did she look like that little lady right there?" the Captain interrupted, pointing at a new arrival to the party. "Ahoy, Len, over here!" he brayed, waving a hand in the air.

When Ketch turned to see who he was pointing at, his face turned even redder than it had when the Captain had ribbed him about Kari. He lowered his head and sipped at his beer.

"Hey, Don," Len said to the Captain. Some of the others at the picnic table had gotten up and left, so Len plopped down on the bench next to Ketch. "Hey Ketch, how you doin'?" he said. Ketch noticed that, like the Captain, Len was not costumed, though the bib overalls and straw hat he typically wore would still qualify him if there were a contest. The girl Len had brought with him sat down by the Captain.

"Guess I ought to introduce everybody," Len declared. "This here is Cap'n Don, and this here is Ketch," he said to the girl. "Storm Ketchum is his real name, but don't call him that less'n you want your head bit off," he added with a typically goofy grin. "Don and Ketch, this here is –"

"I know!" the Captain exclaimed. "The ghost a Cora the witch, right?"

"Huh?" Len responded, perplexed.

The girl laughed. "I'm Diana. Mister Ketchum, it's nice to meet you – again," she said. "Len, this is the man I told you I spoke with back at the Cora Tree, while I was waitin' on you to pick me up."

Then Len understood. "Well, how 'bout that!" he said. "Small world, ain't it? Yeah, she's stayin' at a place right by that tree." He slapped Ketch on the back, almost causing him to spill his beer. "I guess she got you pretty good back there, huh? She's kind of a practical joker, in case y'all didn't know."

"Well, we know now," the Captain said. "Ketch told me all about it. Hey Ketch, what's the matter? You look like you seen a ghost!" he guffawed. "I'm sorry, I shouldn't a laughed," he apologized to Ketch.

"That's okay," Ketch finally said. "I can take a joke," he added, though the brooding look on his face wasn't yet supporting that statement.

"Did you really think I was Cora's ghost?" Diana asked Ketch.

"Well no, not really, that is, not after I'd thought about it," Ketch stammered.

"Mister Ketchum – Ketch – I'm truly sorry if I alarmed you," Diana said. "But when I saw you lookin' for the name on that tree all serious like, and lookin' nervous and all there in the dark, I just couldn't resist, and –"

"Where did you go at the end, when you disappeared?" Ketch interrupted.

"Oh! Well, I just ducked around the other side of the tree and hunkered down."

"I see," Ketch stiffly responded.

"I'm truly sorry, really," Diana repeated. "It's just a bad habit of mine, playin' jokes on people. I've been doin' it since I was a kid."

Ketch exhaled loudly. "That's all right," he said. "Really, no hard feelings." He finally allowed himself a smile. One should be able to laugh at oneself, right? He'd read somewhere that it was a positive character trait, and he was trying to improve himself after all, so he decided to let his embarrassment go. "What kind of accent were you using when we talked?" he pleasantly inquired. "I thought maybe it was Hoi Toider at first."

"It's supposed to be some kind of eighteenth-century Tidewater accent. I worked up at Colonial Williamsburg in Virginia over the summer, and they taught it to us there."

"Well, that explains that, then," Ketch said. He got up from the bench. "Can I get you something to drink?" he asked her. "I don't know what there is besides beer, though. Captain?"

"There's wine and margaritas and such inside, if you want that kinda thing."

"I'll walk with you," Diana said. "And we'll bring some beers back for y'all." She got up, went to Ketch, and crooked an arm inside his elbow. "That is, if you do not mind it, kind sir," she added with a chuckle.

Ketch let out a rueful chuckle in return. "You really did have me going there for a while," he admitted as they made their way to the drinks.

"I did, didn't I?" she giggled. "I'm studyin' to be an actress in my spare time, you know, so it was a confidence booster for me, at least. But meanwhile, I'm workin' at HatterasMann Realty. What do you do?"

"I retired almost three years ago. Now I mate on the Captain's charters and help teach scuba classes."

"You're retired? You must have retired young!"

"Well, I was fifty-five, but I don't think that's very young..."

After getting everyone a round of drinks, he spent some more time with the Captain, Len, and Diana. And then, as he was realizing he was hungry and considering going inside for some food, he saw Kari going in – or rather, yet another pirate wench, but he had no trouble recognizing her. He hadn't noticed her arrival, but she couldn't have been here very long. He scanned the surroundings for any sign of Mick, and didn't see him anywhere. Maybe the scoundrel had something, or more likely someone, better to do this evening.

Ketch excused himself and followed Kari into the Captain's condo. There was pizza, subs, a mountain of peel-and-eat shrimp, a couple of veggie platters, and other assorted munchies, all laid out on the dining room table and the kitchen counters. It looked like she was going for the subs, so he joined her there.

"Hello, Kari," he said from behind her.

"Oh, hey Ketch," she said, turning to face him and eyeing his costume. "My, don't you look handsome! In fact, don't we make a handsome couple!" She rotated in place and modeled her costume for him. "Do you agree, O Captain?"

How could he not? He had to admit she looked rather fetching, even more so than usual, but how should he phrase that? "Uh, sure, whatever you say," he punted. Why did he always feel like a bashful teenager when he was alone with her? "Um, would you like to join me for dinner?"

"Sure, why not? Let's load up a couple plates and find someplace to sit."

They ended up back at the picnic table with the Captain, Len, Diana, and now Kitty as well. The Captain's new squeeze had brought a large platter out with her, and they all chatted amiably while they ate. This was fine with Ketch, since he didn't have to worry about coming up with topics of conversation, though he did sit next to Kari and pay her as much attention as possible. He unfortunately had to suffer through another recap of his adventure at the Cora Tree, but it was a small price to pay.

When some of the other guests started using the open space on the deck as a dance floor, Ketch was afraid Kari might ask him to dance. But she didn't, and instead declared that she had to be at the shop early in the morning. Being the gentleman that he was, he walked her out to her car.

"That was a funny joke Diana played on you," she said. "Kinda cruel too, but still funny, you gotta admit. Hey, don't feel bad," she said, seeing the look on his face. "That would have scared the bejesus out of me, even worse than it did you. I would have headed for the hills as fast as these ole feet would take me!"

"There aren't too many hills around here,

except for the sand dunes," he said with a smile. "It's okay, I'm over it."

"You sure? Good. Hey, c'mere." She gave him a quick hug before he realized what was happening, and then got in her car. "There's an Open Water class startin' Monday, probably my last one for the year. Will you be available for the pool work?" Ketch assured her that he would. "Great! I really appreciate you helpin' out, I hope you know that. Okay then," she said, starting the engine, "goodnight!"

After she left, Ketch stuck around a little while longer to be polite. But with Kari gone, he no longer had much of an incentive to stay, and the party was starting to grow rowdier than he was comfortable with. So he made his rounds and said his goodbyes.

It was going on midnight when he finally left the party. He hadn't had that much to drink, and he'd stopped drinking a couple hours ago and eaten some food as well, so he wasn't worried about driving his truck. He'd just have to keep an eye out for the small deer that lived in Buxton Woods.

This time he allowed himself to fully enjoy the night sky, as well as the wanly illuminated subtropical scenery along the way, which tonight ranged from ocean views to sound views and maritime forest (and a few houses and other buildings, which he mostly ignored). Although the moon was still almost full, more stars were visible here on this clear night than he'd ever seen back North. There was less light pollution here than anyplace he'd ever lived, outside of the village centers anyway. Being thirty miles out to sea on a barrier island also meant no light to speak of from the mainland.

But still, as he approached Brigands' Bay in Frisco, he felt strangely compelled to revisit the Cora Tree. It was midnight. Might he see something out of the ordinary if he went back there now, on this night when the spirts of the departed were said to roam the Earth? Did he *want* to see something that was extraordinary in that way? He'd never been able to embrace any religion the way so many others did so facilely, but did he nonetheless feel a need to find something bigger than himself to believe in?

Maybe... It wouldn't be unusual to feel that way, since most people apparently did, and had throughout history. But didn't he already have that, in the form of the glorious Nature that was all around him here? He'd never before in his life felt the kind of peace and happiness that the island and the sea around it were bringing him now. Being a part, however minuscule and ephemeral, of the beautifully complex and ever-evolving ecosystems of this island and the others nearby, and the waters that surrounded them, and appreciating all of that with the reverence it so richly deserved – wasn't that believing in something? And wasn't it big enough, and extraordinary enough?

He decided that it was, for now anyway. He drove past the Buccaneer Drive turnoff without slowing, and continued on home to *Port Starbird* – where his trusty canine companion was probably missing him, and perhaps crossing his legs, by now. If Cora and her tree had any supernatural secrets to reveal, they would have to wait for another time.

~ *The End* ~

Thanks for reading this story! I hope you enjoyed it. If you did, and if you have time, please consider taking a few minutes to post a short review online. Reviews help increase an independently published book's visibility, and I'd greatly appreciate it. Thanks again!

Keep a weather eye out for the next Storm Ketchum Tale! You might also enjoy Ketch's full-length Adventures, if you haven't already read them. All Tales and Adventures are available at

www.GarrettDennis.com

While you're there, subscribe to my infrequent newsletter and get a free e-book!